Sinbad
and the
Giant Spider

by Martin Waddell and O'Kif

W

F **'**S

First published in 2010 by
Franklin Watts
338 Euston Road
London
NW1 3BH

Franklin Watts Australia
Level 17/207 Kent Street
Sydney
NSW 2000

Text © Martin Waddell 2010
Illustrations © O'Kif 2010

A CIP catalogue record for this book is available
from the British Library.

ISBN 978 0 7496 9441 8 (hbk)
ISBN 978 0 7496 9447 0 (pbk)

Series Editor: Jackie Hamley
Series Advisor: Catherine Glavina
Series Designer: Peter Scoulding

JS

Printed in China

Franklin Watts is a division of
Hachette Children's Books,
an Hachette UK company
www.hachette.co.uk

One day, Sinbad's ship was attacked by a huge octopus. Sinbad and his friend Ali dived into the churning sea to escape.

Stormy waves cast Sinbad
among needle-sharp rocks
at the foot of a cliff.

He clung to a rock as the waves
smashed against the cliff face.
"Save me, Sinbad!" screamed Ali.

Sinbad pulled Ali out of the sea.
"We're trapped!" groaned Ali.
"We can't climb up that cliff. And
there's no other way out of here."

"There *is* a way,"
said Sinbad.

They dived in and swam down
underwater into the mouth of
the cave beneath the cliff face.

9

Inside the cave, they found
themselves on a beach covered
with sticks white as bone.

"I see daylight up there!" Ali panted.
"If we clamber up from one ledge
to another, we can escape."

11

They started the steep climb from
the depths of the cave. Each time
they reached a new ledge,
there were more piles of sticks
with sharp, broken edges.
"Oh no!" Sinbad groaned.

13

"Those aren't sticks!" Sinbad said grimly. "They're bones! Bones that have been broken and chewed. Something man-eating lives here!"

"Wha-wha-what sort of something?" stammered Ali. "That sort of something!" said Sinbad the Sailor.

"A Giant Man-Eating Spider is on
his way down for a Sinbad-and-Ali
packed lunch!" wailed Ali.
"How do we get out of this?"

"Think, think, THINK!" Sinbad
said. And he thought...

And he thought...

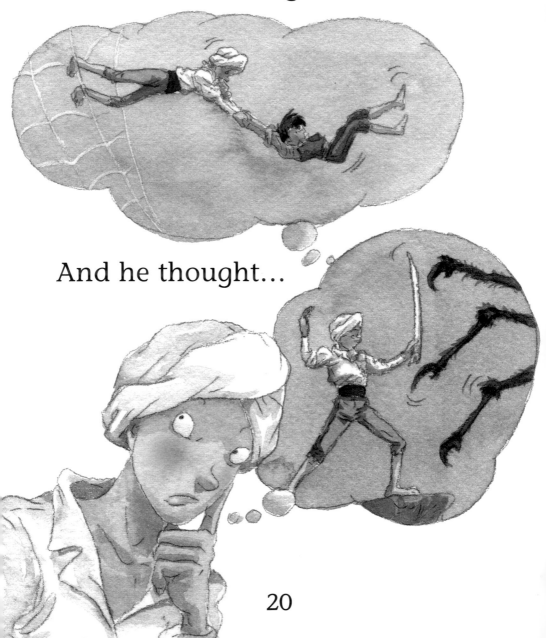

20

"You dance and shout to attract the spider while I play hide-and-snip with this sharp-edged bone!" grinned Sinbad.

Sinbad hid stone-still in the shadows as the spider spun down towards the dancing and shouting Ali. Then...

Sinbad and Ali scrambled out of
the cave at the top of the cliff.

Spider's Cave

DANGER

of death

"Heroes-are-us!" laughed Sinbad,
and everyone cheered.

Sinbad and Ali sailed home (first class) with sacks full of gold.

"Well...er... spun, Ali!" laughed
Sinbad the Sailor.

Puzzle 1

Put these pictures in the correct order.
Which event do you think is most important?
Now try writing the story in your own words!

Puzzle 2

1. This is a bone, not a stick!

2. You've saved our village!

3. Come here, Giant Spider!

4. Is there something up there, Sinbad?

5. I can cut the web with this bone.

6. That spider has been scaring us for years!

Choose the correct speech bubbles for the characters above. Can you think of any others? Turn over to find the answers.

Answers

Puzzle 1

The correct order is: 1d, 2a, 3e, 4f, 5b, 6c

Puzzle 2

Ali: 3, 4

Sinbad: 1, 5

The villagers: 2, 6

Look out for more Hopscotch Adventures:

TALES OF KING ARTHUR

1. The Sword in the Stone
ISBN 978 0 7496 6694 1

2. Arthur the King
ISBN 978 0 7496 6695 8

3. The Round Table
ISBN 978 0 7496 6697 2

4. Sir Lancelot and the Ice Castle
ISBN 978 0 7496 6698 9

5. Sir Gawain and the Green Knight
ISBN 978 0 7496 8557 7*
ISBN 978 0 7496 8569 0

6. Sir Galahad and the Holy Grail
ISBN 978 0 7496 8558 4*
ISBN 978 0 7496 8570 6

TALES OF ROBIN HOOD

Robin and the Knight
ISBN 978 0 7496 6699 6

Robin and the Monk
ISBN 978 0 7496 6700 9

Robin and the Silver Arrow
ISBN 978 0 7496 6703 0

Robin and the Friar
ISBN 978 0 7496 6702 3

Robin and the Butcher
ISBN 978 0 7496 8555 3*
ISBN 978 0 7496 8568 3

Robin and Maid Marian
ISBN 978 0 7496 8556 0*
ISBN 978 0 7496 8567 6

TALES OF SINBAD THE SAILOR

Sinbad and the Ogre
ISBN 978 0 7496 8559 1*
ISBN 978 0 7496 8571 3

Sinbad and the Whale
ISBN 978 0 7496 8553 9*
ISBN 978 0 7496 8565 2

Sinbad and the Diamond Valley
ISBN 978 0 7496 8554 6*
ISBN 978 0 7496 8566 9

Sinbad and the Monkeys
ISBN 978 0 7496 8560 7*
ISBN 978 0 7496 8572 0

Sinbad and the Giant Spider
ISBN 978 0 7496 9441 8*
ISBN 978 0 7496 9447 0

Sinbad and the Pirates
ISBN 978 0 7496 9442 5*
ISBN 978 0 7496 9448 7

For more *Hopscotch Adventures* **and other** *Hopscotch* **stories, visit:**
www.franklinwatts.co.uk

* hardback